THE BOOK OF
DRAGONS
SECRETS OF
THE DRAGON DOMAIN

S. A. CALDWELL

CARLTON KIDS

CONTENTS

DRAGONS ARE EVERYWHERE.

THEY ARE THE ROARING OF THE WIND, A FLICKER IN THE NIGHT SKY, A RUSTLING IN THE FOREST. THEY ARE THE GLINT BENEATH A DESERT SUN, A STIRRING IN STILL WATERS, THE FURY IN THE EYE OF A STORM.

THROUGH THE AGES, man has tried to understand and tame the mighty dragon. Few have seen this extraordinary animal, yet its name is known to all. Dragons inhabit every part of our world, and yet remain as mysterious as ever. What exactly is this fabulous beast we call the dragon?

This is the question that has long burned in my heart. The book you hold in your hands is a labor of love, the fruit of a lifetime's inquiry and many years of research.

My quest has taken me to Earth's remotest places—to rocky mountain ranges and vast deserts; to dark, ancient forests and desolate, frozen landscapes. Yet the greatest challenge has been to open my mind to the impossible, for dragons defy the ordinary. As you turn these pages, prepare for the unknown, the incredible, and the unearthly.

Perhaps most astonishing for the reader are the collections displayed here for the first time. Marvel at the Drachenfels teeth, buried for almost a thousand years in ancient castle ruins before their chance discovery, or the magnificent claw specimens gathered from the farthest corners of the world. Many have warned of the perils of owning any part of a dragon. These collectors risk all to increase knowledge of this beast. We owe them much.

No one can ever know the dragon fully. So it has always been, and so it will remain. My wish is that these pages bring you a little closer to understanding these strange and wonderful creatures.

S. A. CALDWELL
The Ancient Guild of Dragon Research

A World of DRAGONS

Dragons can be found across the far reaches of our world. They are masters of the skies, soaring majestically over scorching deserts or frozen lands. They swoop from glittering peaks in a blaze of fire or arise from the depths of the Earth. Some slither serpent-like through rivers and lakes, ascending to the clouds in a flash of lightning, while others lurk silently in ancient forests.

Dragons are as varied as the realms they inhabit. Our world is also their own...

Dragon Realms
A Study of Habitats

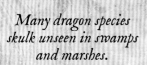

Many dragon species skulk unseen in swamps and marshes.

DRAGONS MAKE THEIR LAIRS in an astonishing range of places. They can be divided into seven main types according to habitat: mountain, woodland, grassland, freshwater, swamp, polar and desert. A very few species live in the ocean, but most cannot thrive in salt water.

Extreme Environments
Rare dragons may be found in habitats that would challenge any other animal. For example, the Laki Lava Dragon of Iceland lives among hot, bubbling geysers, and can survive lakes of molten lava.

Dragon Variety
As with all Earth's creatures, dragons have adapted to live successfully in their habitats. Ice dragons, with almost translucent silvery scales, blend seamlessly into snowy landscapes, while the nocturnal Flaming Humped Dragon of north Africa escapes the scorching desert sun by hiding away in its underground lair during daylight hours. The eyes, ears, and nostrils of swamp dragons lie across the top of their heads, allowing them to lurk for many hours just beneath the surface of foul-smelling swamps, watching and waiting for tasty morsels to pass their way.

The Barb-tailed Savannah Dragon of Africa scans open grassland for its prey.

THE ROUGH MOUNTAIN TERRAIN OF THE
SNAGGLE~TOOTHED
MOUNTAIN DRAGON

Mountain dragons are agile and surefooted,
allowing them to clamber nimbly over rugged terrain.

Glacier Cave of the Antarctic Snow Dragon

This magnificent creature has rarely been seen by human eyes. Found in frozen Antarctica, it spends days at a time in its icy lair during the long, dark winter. When hungry, it emerges to skim the Antarctic sea, diving into its depths for orcas and large seals.

Dragon Gallery

A Study of Species

So varied and numerous are dragon species that it would be impossible to show them all on these pages. Here are six dragons from different habitats to represent the dazzling variety of dragonkind.

The Snaggle-toothed Mountain Dragon makes its lair at high altitude in central and eastern Europe. Like other mountain species, it has excellent eyesight. Its misaligned teeth are still vicious in attack.

The Razor-fanged Marsh Dragon is found mainly in southern Asia and is a threat to passing birds, deer, buffalo, and even humans. This species cannot fly, but it is very nimble on dry land.

The Pygmy Forest Dragon

lives at the heart of north America's vast forests. Although no bigger than an antelope, this agile and muscular dragon includes bears and mountain lions in its diet.

The Five-clawed Serpent Dragon

lives in the rivers and lakes of eastern Asia. Although wingless, it can soar to the clouds. It is remarkably intelligent and can transform into many guises.

The Crystal Ice Dragon

soars through the skies of northern polar lands and breathes blasts of icy air to stun its prey of polar bears, musk oxen, and moose. Its pearl-like scales are almost translucent.

The Triple-horned Night Dragon

is a rare species found in the Outback of Australia. Notable for its spine-chilling, wolf-like howl, this dragon leaves its lair only in darkness.

Anatomy
of the
Dragon

Whether blazing across starry skies or slithering through murky waters, a dragon is one of the most imposing sights in all of nature. The variety found among dragonkind is breathtaking. All species possess unique bodily forms that set them apart from other creatures.

From all-seeing eyes to the ability to breathe fire or ice, a dragon's features are a source of constant wonder.

THROUGH THE AGES, DRAGONS' AMAZING SKELETONS HAVE MYSTIFIED THOSE WHO STUDY THEM.

DRAGON BONES ARE AS STRONG AS IRON TO SUPPORT THIS CREATURE'S MIGHTY BULK. AND YET THEY ARE AS LIGHT AND HOLLOW AS THE BONES OF A BIRD, GIVING THE DRAGON THE GIFT OF FLIGHT.

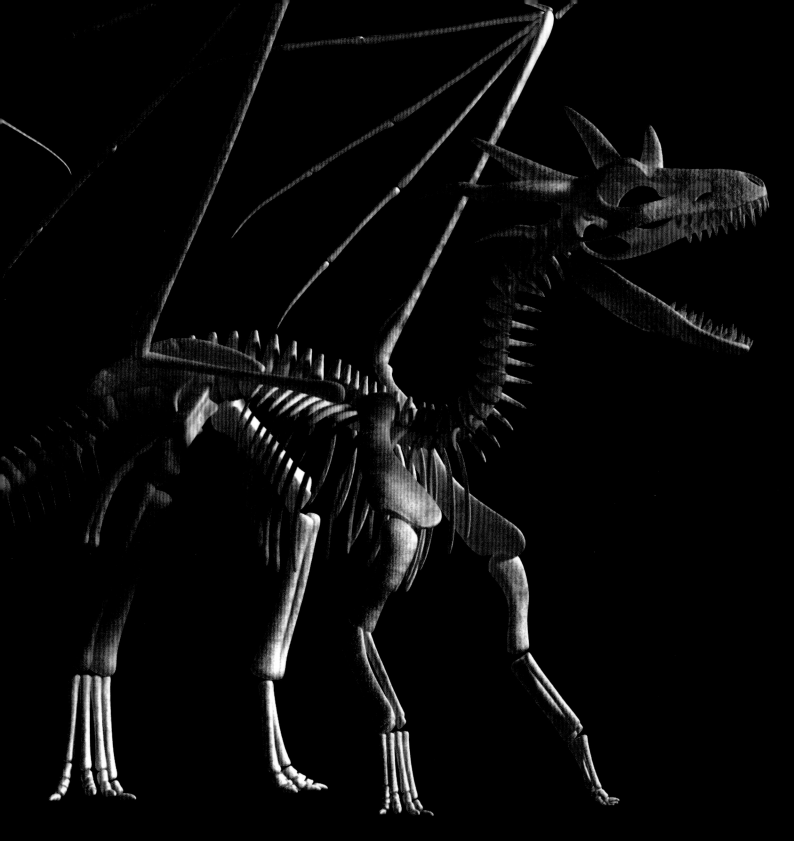

The SICKLE-CLAWED FOREST DRAGON *has protective thorn-like eyelashes.*

A "second eye"—a translucent, protective covering—allows some dragons to see underwater.

The BLACK BOG DRAGON *has a uniquely-shaped eye pupil.*

The TRIPLE-HORNED NIGHT DRAGON *'s pupil is vertical.*

THE DRAGON'S SENSES

A STUDY OF SIGHT, HEARING & SMELL

MUCH HAS BEEN WRITTEN of the dragon's astonishing eyesight. Our own vision is so poor by comparison that it is hard to imagine the world as dragons see it. They can observe a scene many miles away in perfect focus and vivid color. Their night vision is exceptional, too.

DANGEROUS VISION

Dragon eyes come in every imaginable hue, from forest-green and sky-blue, to copper, bronze, and burnished gold. But beware: to look into a dragon's eyes is foolhardy. Its stare has the effect of placing the viewer in a trance from which they are unlikely to recover.

UNEARTHLY PERCEPTION

Although not in the same league as their eyesight, a dragon's hearing and sense of smell are not to be underestimated. Dragons can discern sounds well outside the human range, and have been known to respond to courting calls over fifty miles away. Similarly, dragons can detect and decode scents carried on the wind over vast distances. Although barely understood, it is clear that dragons also possess a sixth sense, enabling them to seek out gold and precious stones hidden from view.

THE HOOK-BEAKED MOUNTAIN DRAGON

The Hook-beaked Mountain Dragon's senses make it a terrifying predator. Its eyes can pinpoint victims many miles away, while its acute hearing and incredible sense of smell mean that it can detect prey even when hidden.

Beware the
glint in a
dragon's eye:

Cold as ice to
the liar,

Sharp as a
knife to the
knave,

Hard as iron
to the greedy,

A burning
flame to the
brave.

THE DRACHENFELS TEETH

 uried for nearly a thousand years, this collection of dragon teeth was discovered in a secret vault below ancient castle ruins. It is said to be dangerous to own any part of a dragon. He who made the find met a most mysterious end...
The teeth shown here demonstrate the savage power of a dragon's jaws. The ferocious canine of the Saber-fanged Mountain Dragon is the length of a man's arm, and the largest specimen of its kind. Canines are used to grasp prey and pierce flesh, while razor-sharp incisors slice through skin and tear meat from bones. Dragons that do not swallow their prey whole have bone-crushing molars for grinding down any indigestible elements of their meal.

Horned Desert Dragon

Razor-fanged Marsh Dragon

Crystal Ice Dragon

Black Bog Dragon

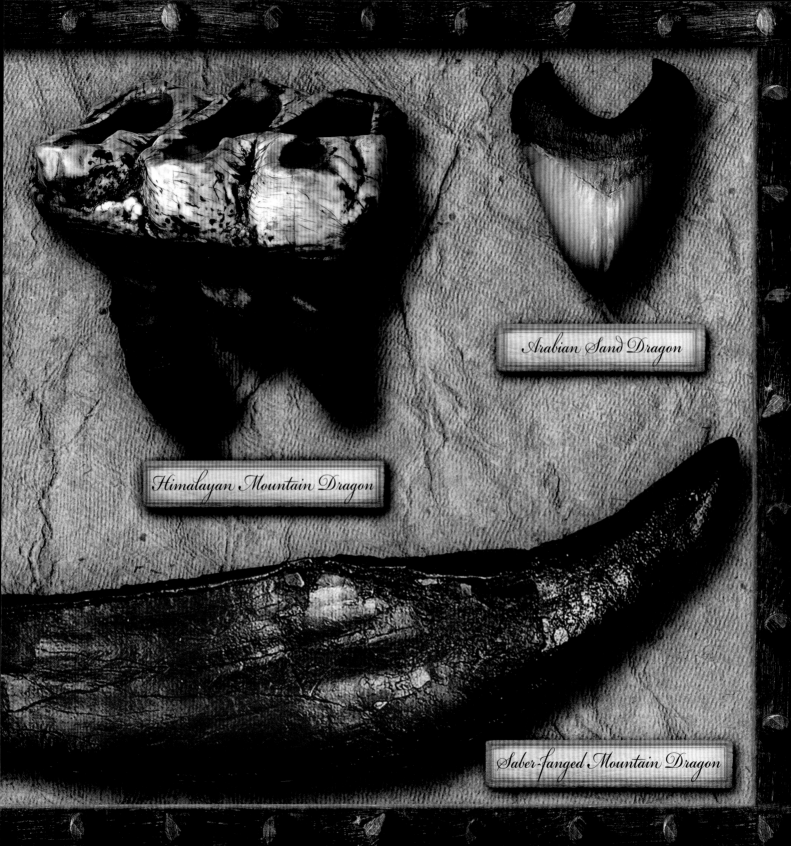

Arabian Sand Dragon

Himalayan Mountain Dragon

Saber-Fanged Mountain Dragon

SCALES OF THE WYRM TREASURY

Drawn from the darkest corners of the Earth, this collection of dragon scales is the pride of the Wyrm Treasury in Krakow, Poland. Legend has it that the scales will burst into flames if used to make evil spells against dragonkind.

Scale samples of this size fall away from a dragon's body throughout its long life but are very rarely found. From the burning heat of the Vulcanian Fire Dragon to the frosty touch of the Black Ice Dragon, all scale samples preserve the temperature of the bodies of their original hosts.

Siberian Frost Dragon

Burnished Water Dragon

Vulcanian Fire Dragon

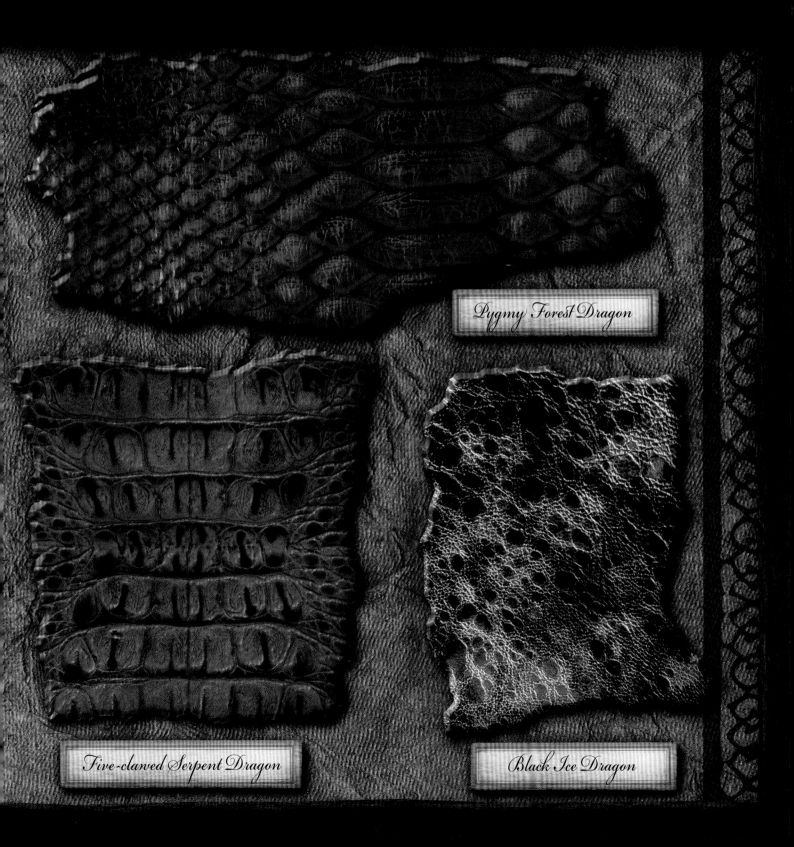

Pygmy Forest Dragon

Five-clawed Serpent Dragon

Black Ice Dragon

Dragon Claws
A Study of Talons

A DRAGON'S CLAWS OR TALONS must surely rank as one of this creature's greatest weapons. Ancient tales tell of claws slicing through a slayer's armor as easily as oars cutting through water.

Dragons typically have three or four talons on each hand or foot, though some water dragons have five. Claws may also be found on the wing tips of some species. Tougher than diamonds, dragon claws are made of a material otherwise unknown in the natural world. They are highly prized by sorcerers, who grind them to a glittering powder for use in spells.

The hooked claws of the BARB-TAILED SAVANNAH DRAGON.

The short claws of the HORNED SWAMP DRAGON.

The five talons of the FIVE-CLAWED SERPENT DRAGON.

DAGGER-SHARP WEAPONS

A dragon's claws must be kept in prime condition at all times. Tree trunks and other rough surfaces may be used for sharpening, and broken claws are quick to heal. A dragon will retract its talons when moving on hard ground to prevent damage and to stop clattering claws alerting prey.

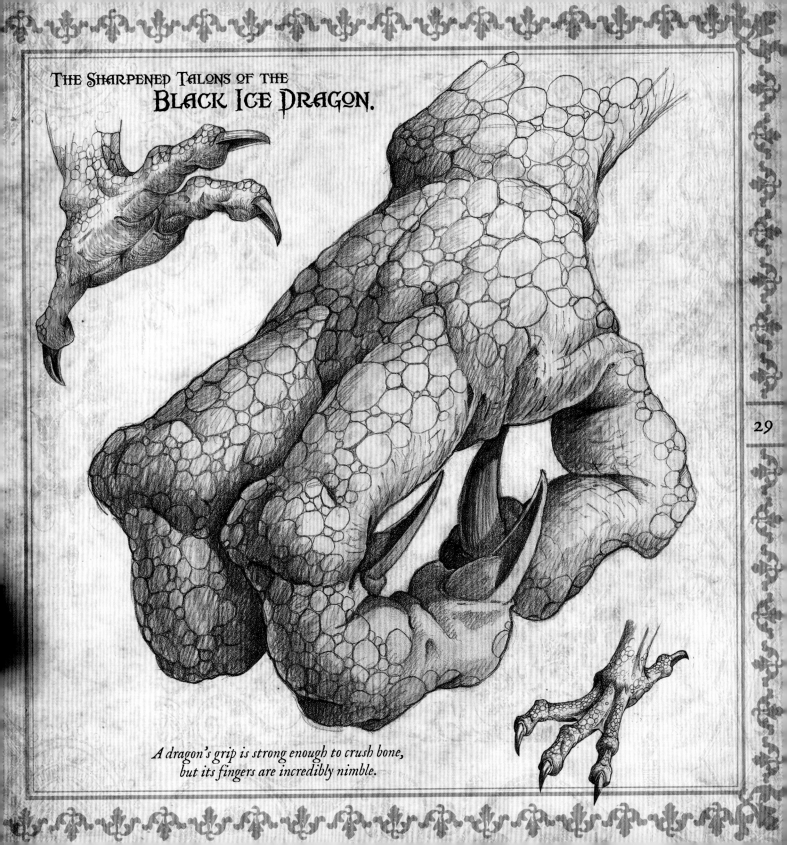

THE SHARPENED TALONS OF THE
BLACK ICE DRAGON.

A dragon's grip is strong enough to crush bone,
but its fingers are incredibly nimble.

Horns & Tails
Deadly Weapons
in the Dragon's Armory

The multiple horns of the
RED PRAIRIE DRAGON.

A DRAGON'S HORNS OR ANTLERS can prove devastating in both attack and defense. From the lethal spikes of the Bearded Mountain Dragon to the spiral antlers of many serpent dragons or the woody stumps of the Sickle-clawed Forest Dragon, a startling variety of horns and antlers are seen across dragon species.

Horns are made of bone and grow continuously from the dragon's skull, often reaching a quite staggering size. By contrast, antlers are shed yearly and are much desired by sorcerers for their magical properties. Dragons use their horns and antlers to gore prey, and to win a mate in the breeding season, when males often fight to the death. It goes without saying that two dragons locking horns in mortal combat is a terrifying spectacle.

The spiked horns of the
BEARDED MOUNTAIN DRAGON.

A horn belonging to the ARABIAN SAND DRAGON.

The curved antlers of the
BURNISHED WATER DRAGON.

TERRIBLE TAILS
The tail is the dragon's secret weapon—a single lash may well prove deadly. Tails can be forked or arrow-tipped, spiked, or end in a bone-crushing club. Some species, such as the usually peaceful Five-clawed Serpent Dragon, when attacked can use their tails to squeeze the life from a victim.

THE CHARACTERISTIC FEATURES OF
DRAGON TAILS

The spiked tail of the Horned Swamp Dragon can inflict dire injury on its prey.

The feathered tail of the Arabian Sand Dragon.

Though it seems delicate, the tail of the Fan-tailed Desert Dragon is very strong.

The long, muscular tail of the Five-clawed Serpent Dragon can suffocate a victim.

The unique tail of the Sickle-clawed Forest Dragon.

Wings of the Pike Collection

---

hese incredibly rare wing fragments form part of the private collection of the world-renowned dragon hunter Dr. Tiberius Pike. Quite how he chanced upon these beautifully preserved specimens remains a mystery, but a team of experts has confirmed their authenticity.

Laki Lava Dragon

Thought to be at least a hundred years old, this copper-red wing fragment comes from the Laki Lava Dragon of Iceland. Known to have survived the great Laki volcanic eruption of 1783, this species can tolerate incredible extremes of temperature. Dragon wings are thin yet amazingly strong. This wing sample is covered with a curious fire-resistant layer, which is unknown elsewhere in the natural world.

CRYSTAL ICE DRAGON

Preserved in Antarctic ice, this paper-thin wing fragment is believed to be over three thousand years old. The wing specimen was discovered next to the similarly preserved thumb claw of the ferocious Black Ice Dragon. It is possible that these two dragons were engaged in mortal combat when they met their deaths.

Thumb Claw of the
Black Ice Dragon

DRAGON FIRE

Through the centuries, many have tried to explain the dragon's remarkable ability to exhale scorching flames. Not all dragons are fire-breathers, but those that are possess a terrible weapon. A single blast usually results in instant death for the victim. What causes this extraordinary phenomenon?

SOLVING THE RIDDLE

Experts now believe that the element phosphorus is the answer to this great mystery. All creatures need phosphorus to survive, but it is thought that chemical reactions within the dragon's body create the pure form, white phosphorus. Extremely flammable, white phosphorus instantly ignites on exposure to air when cheek glands pass the element into the dragon's mouth. Phosphorus traces found in the wake of dragon fire provide tantalizing evidence to support this theory.

The Way of the Dragon

The secrets of dragonkind have puzzled and intrigued us through the ages. It is thought that dragons live for between a thousand and ten thousand years, but can we be sure? No dragon life has ever been studied in its entirety.

The observations on the following pages must be viewed as fragments of the whole picture. From birth to death, there is much in the dragon's way of life that remains cloaked in mystery.

A hatchling
GOLDEN FIRE DRAGON.

The adolescent
GOLDEN FIRE DRAGON.

The mature
GOLDEN FIRE DRAGON.

AGES OF THE DRAGON
FROM BIRTH TO DEATH

SOME HAVE CLAIMED that most baby dragons remain in their eggs for three thousand years before hatching —a thousand in the ocean depths, a thousand on icy mountain peaks, and a thousand warmed by the sun.

STONES OF LIFE
Depending on the species, an adult female lays between one and a hundred eggs. Eggs come in all shapes and sizes, and may be mistaken for beautiful stones. Baby dragons are said to make a high-pitched "singing" sound as hatching time approaches. Hatchlings emerge from their shells with the aid of an egg tooth at the end of their snouts, and at least one parent is present to greet them. If danger threatens, or in extreme cold, the young may be carried inside their mother's mouth.

FROM HATCHLING TO DRAGON
Baby dragons resemble their parents in almost every respect, though their scales are soft, their horns undeveloped, and their eyesight lacks the adult's telescopic power. In serpent species, ancient writings report wriggling hatchlings growing to full size within minutes. However, for most the path to adulthood is thought to take several hundred years.

A Dragon's Old Age

As a dragon's final centuries approach, its body begins to show signs of aging. Elderly dragons become gnarled in appearance, bright scales turn dull, and teeth and claws take on a yellow hue. As energy levels decrease and senses become less acute, these aged beasts are less inclined to travel far, and may become bad tempered. However, despite losing physical strength, ancient dragons have extraordinary wisdom and are revered throughout the dragon kingdom.

Warts and bumps may appear, and eyes grow sunken.

The tail has a ragged, moth-eaten appearance.

The wing claw is chipped and shows signs of yellowing.

THE SUMATRAN
EGG COLLECTION

Very closely guarded on Sumatra, "The Island of Gold", the six dragon eggs of this curious collection are known to make a gentle humming sound when gathered together in one place.

1. ARABIAN SAND DRAGON
2. KRAKATOAN LAVA DRAGON
3. SUMATRAN WATER DRAGON
4. TRIPLE-HORNED NIGHT DRAGON
5. ANTARCTIC SNOW DRAGON
6. BEARDED MOUNTAIN DRAGON

1.

4.

Food and Hunting

All dragons are meat-eaters, though many enjoy plant-based foods, too. The Copper-breasted Marsh Dragon of subtropical America is particularly fond of the blood berry plant, while the Long-snouted Water Dragon of southern Europe supplements its diet with the deadly mandrake root, poisonous to most animals.

The Dragon's Deathly Blows

Dragons employ a wide variety of methods to kill their prey. Many swoop down from on high with claws extended, and either carry off their prey or consume it on the spot. Species living on open plains stalk their prey before bursting into a swift pursuit that is over in a matter of seconds. Many wetland species lurk just beneath the surface of a swamp or marsh, rearing up to snatch a passing victim with razor-sharp fangs. Some species rely solely on fire-breathing to scorch their prey, while dragons living in snowy lands breathe out blasts of icy air to stun a victim.

SUPER SENSES

A few species use unusual hunting techniques. Emerging only in darkness, the Australian Triple-horned Night Dragon places an ear to the ground and is able to sense dingo from a vast distance. The Amazonian Water Dragon preys on the giant anaconda snake. Tiny hairs on the underside of this dragon's tail detect minute vibrations from the reptile even many miles away.

Horned Desert Dragon

Horned Swamp Dragon

Burnished Water Dragon

Golden Fire Dragon

Great African Ram Dragon

THE DRAKON EXPEDITION

Assembled by a famous team of dragon specialists, this spectacular array of claws is the result of an expedition visiting five continents and some of the wildest places on Earth. The team crossed vast stretches of forest, desert, and ice, scaled craggy peaks and plunged into underground caverns. One life was lost, and one expert is missing still.

CLAW VARIETY

These claws testify to the sheer variety of dragonkind. Behold the curved barb of the Hook-clawed Mountain Dragon or the vicious claw of the Flat-snouted Night Dragon. The claw of the Horned Desert Dragon shown here is a wing claw. This terrifying predator uses the talons on each wing tip in aerial battles with rival dragons.

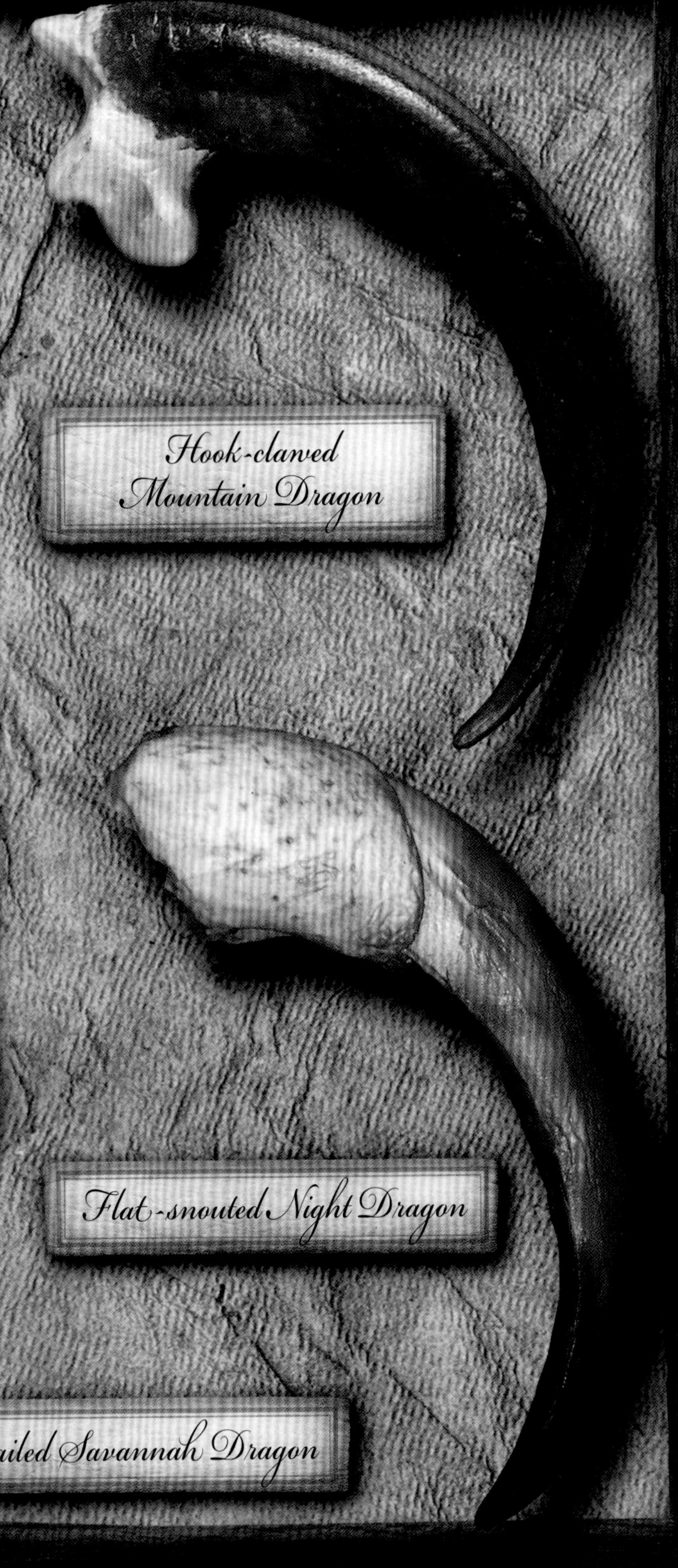

Hook-clawed
Mountain Dragon

Flat-snouted Night Dragon

Barb-tailed Savannah Dragon

The Dragon Lair
A Study of Caves, Nests & Burrows

Sandstone rocks shelter the lairs of desert dragons.

MORE THAN A NESTING SITE, the dragon's lair is its refuge. In deep, dark caves, on soaring cliff ledges, in riverbank burrows and hollowed-out trees, dragon lairs are as varied as dragons themselves. Beware! A dragon guards its lair with its life!

Yawning Caves

Many dragons choose inky-black caves that offer space and solitude—the dragon is secretive by its very nature. Some species have been known to inhabit giant crystal caves, deep underground. Too hot for any other living creature, these glittering chambers attract treasure-loving dragons. Species living in the frozen polar lands find glacier caves. Most dragons settle in one lair for life, but ice dragons may move as glaciers shift or melt.

The Dragon's Hoard

The dragon's love of treasure is well known, although some dragons are cleverer than others at finding precious gems. Nearly all lairs contain a collection of stones—whether sparkling sapphires or simple shiny pebbles. Those who risk their lives to gain a dragon's hoard are disappointed by the latter.

This gold nugget once belonged to an Arabian Sand Dragon.

Nests, Burrows and Holes

Some mountain dragons make their nests high on remote and rugged cliffs. They choose windy areas, where updrafts help them to gain height even while carrying heavy prey. Smaller species, such as woodland dragons, make nests in treetops, or in hollowed-out tree trunks. Grassland dragons may simply scratch a hole in the soil, but the Black Dwarf Dragon burrows underground, creating elaborate tunnels, and many water species dig simple holes in riverbanks.

Dragons living in snowy lands seek refuge in ice caves.

Caves and caverns are ideal for larger mountain species.

A hollow tree trunk is perfect for small woodland species.

To he who seeks the dragon's lair
   And prizes rich beyond compare,
Rubies red and glittering gold,
   Pray heed these words of ages old:

———

Should such treasures fill
your purse,
Beware the power of a
dragon's curse!

DRACHENFELS

High on jagged rocks that overlook the German Rhineland, a ruined castle sits. Legend tells that it was here that Siegfried slew the dragon Fafnir. Afterward, Siegfried roasted the beast's heart and drank its blood. This gave him understanding of the speech of birds.

Dragons are strangely drawn to this mystical site, known as Drachenfels. Hiding in their lairs by day, they emerge only under cover of darkness. On a still, moonlit night, some say you may hear the soft beat of a wing, or glimpse shadowy forms circling the craggy rocks.

Legend
and Lore

Dragons have always stalked this world. Ancient writings and legends tell of these fearsome creatures — horrifying accounts of monstrous beasts, tales of courage and valor, stories of magic and mystery.

Those who seek to know the dragon must pay heed to the legends and lore of yesteryear — for there is much that remains as mysterious as ever.

Magic and Mystery
Enchantment and Sorcery

The enormous heart of the Bearded Mountain Dragon.

Through the centuries, sorcerers and alchemists have attempted to harness the dragon's powerful magic for their own purposes. Many parts of the dragon are known to possess magical properties, but great care is needed in dealing with dragon parts. Although their magic may be used for good, it can cause terrible harm in the wrong hands.

The Heart

There are those who say a dragon's soul resides in its heart. Dragon slayers from ages past believed that if they plucked out a dragon's heart and consumed it, they would gain the gift of prophecy.

Bones

Dragon bones are thought to have healing qualities. Ground to a fine powder, they are used in spells to treat a wide range of ailments.

Blood

Perhaps the most powerful part of a dragon is its blood. Wizards will go to great lengths to lay hands on this substance, though many fail to understand its full force. Using dragon blood unwisely has disastrous results.

A femur bone from the rear limb of the Golden Fire Dragon.

SCALES

Dragons shed their scales regularly throughout their long lives. There is an extraordinary but little-understood power in these luminous fragments—just one scale held in the palm of the hand will emit a strange pulsating heat. However, beware! All that glitters is not gold.

The fantastical horns of the Great African Ram Dragon.

A shimmering, pearly scale from the Crystal Ice Dragon.

THE TONGUE

Many say that eating a dragon's tongue will give wit, insight and success with words. Dragon tongues are tough and sinewy. They must be eaten at one sitting for these effects to take place.

The long, muscular tongue of the Arabian Sand Dragon.

HORNS

Like dragon bones, ground horns are said to cure illness. To test whether a dragon horn is real, it should be buried in the ground. If it is genuine, a dragon's blood tree—a rare tree with sword-shaped leaves and fiery orange fruits—will spring up at the spot.

OF DRAGON'S BLOOD, I THEE IMPLORE
TO HEED THESE WORDS
FROM ANCIENT LORE.

Drink it, to understand the speech of birds,
Spill it, and you will lose the power of words.

Treasure it, to find the dragon's hoard,
Lose it, and you will perish by the sword.

The Dragon's Pearl

Only the very oldest dragons possess a precious pearl of wisdom. Formed at the beginning of time, these ancient gems are thought to contain moon magic, so that they gleam in the darkness. Many believe these stones contain the wisdom of the stars. He who chances upon a dragon's pearl will be wise indeed...

DRAGON LEGENDS
TALES FROM YESTERYEAR

MANY OF THE DRAGONS that our ancestors feared still roam our world today, but some species have become extinct. They live on in legends told by the fireside. These are stories that all who wish to know more of dragonkind should hear.

MOTHER DRAGON

A very long time ago, an old woman was walking beside a great river when she came across five beautiful stones lying in the grass. She picked them up and took them home. They were so exquisite that she gazed at them many times a day.

One night, there was a terrible storm. As jagged lightning tore the sky and thunder cracked overhead, the stones broke open and five baby dragons crawled out— for the stones were dragon eggs! Quickly, the old lady picked up the serpent- like hatchlings and hurried back to the river, where she released them.

The dragons that lived there were so grateful for the return of their young that they gave the woman the ability to see the future. Wise beyond words, she was known forever afterward as Mother Dragon.

O-GON-CHO, THE GOLDEN DRAGON BIRD

The people of Kyoto in Japan were once plagued by the O-gon-cho, a great white dragon living in a deep, murky lake. Every fifty years, the dragon became a golden songbird with glowing feathers, and rose to the skies. Yet despite its beauty, the people dreaded the O-gon-cho. Its spine-chilling howl tearing through the land foretold famine or disease.

THE WAWEL DRAGON OF KRAKOW

Many centuries ago in Poland, a huge fire-breathing dragon lived in a deep, black cave on Wawel Hill. It terrorized the nearby village, bringing death and destruction. Those who attempted to kill the fearsome beast were scorched to death by its breath. One day, a poor shoemaker's apprentice named Krakus fed a lamb with sulfur and placed it outside the dragon's cave. After eating the lamb, the beast was tortured by a dreadful fire in its belly. It drank and drank from the nearby Vistula river, and swelled terribly until it suddenly burst. There was much rejoicing at the dragon's death, and Krakus was made ruler of the village. Under his wise leadership, the city of Krakow grew up around the hill.

DRAGON SLAYERS

EPIC TALES OF COURAGE AND ADVENTURE

Dragons are revered today, but it was not always so. In ages past, these majestic beasts were feared and provoked into acts of fury. Many have taken up arms against the dragon, but few have emerged victorious. The dragon slayer required wit and bravery to defeat nature's mightiest creature...

WHO DARES TO TAKE THE NAME OF
DRAGON SLAYER?

THE TALES OF SUCH HEROES ARE WRITTEN
IN BLOOD AND LIVE FOREVER MORE.

———————

Hidden in a secret underground vault lie these astonishing relics.
Be warned: the wrath of slain dragons is said to live on in them.

SAINT GEORGE'S SPEAR

This bloodied spear tip comes from the very weapon that Saint George used to battle with the swamp-dwelling dragon of Silene in Libya. This fearsome beast demanded the daily sacrifice of a young woman, and George was determined to slay it. The spear's iron tip has been scratched and damaged, for the dragon's scales were harder than diamonds and resisted George's many blows. The brave warrior was finally able to slay this terrible foe when he plunged his spear into a tiny patch of exposed skin beneath the dragon's wing.

THE BEOWULF TOOTH

This dagger-like tooth is over a thousand years old. It belonged to a frightful dragon that spread terror during the reign of the Anglo-Saxon king Beowulf. When a goblet was stolen from the dragon's glittering hoard, the enraged beast set about scorching the land with its fiery breath. Heroic Beowulf dared to take on this foe, but as he struck the dragon's head, the beast plunged its poisonous fangs into the king's neck. The mortally wounded Beowulf thrust his sword deep into the dragon's heart, before himself falling dead to the ground.

As sharp as the day it was plucked from the slain dragon's jaw, this tooth is said to draw blood from any who touch it.

THE SCALE OF FAFNIR

This glittering scale belonged to none other than Fafnir, a dragon that guarded a hoard of gold many hundreds of years ago. Sigurd, a Norse hero, set out to slay this dreadful beast with a sword so sharp it could slice through iron. He hid himself in a shallow pit near the dragon's lair. When the enormous creature passed over Sigurd's hiding place, the hero drove his sword into its underbelly. He then cut out the dragon's heart and drank its blood.

Still warm to the touch, this scale emits an eerie red glow, and is said to lightly quiver if held in the hand.

Ah! Who would seek
      the dragon's lair
Or meet the dragon's
      fearsome stare?

And who would face
      a dragon's jaws,
Its sharpened teeth,
      its savage claws?

Which one would risk
      a dragon's breath,
The fiery heat
      of certain death?

Or seek to find
      the dragon's pearl,
And all the knowledge
      in the world?

That one is brave,
      I know it well,
But wise to try?
      Pray who can tell?

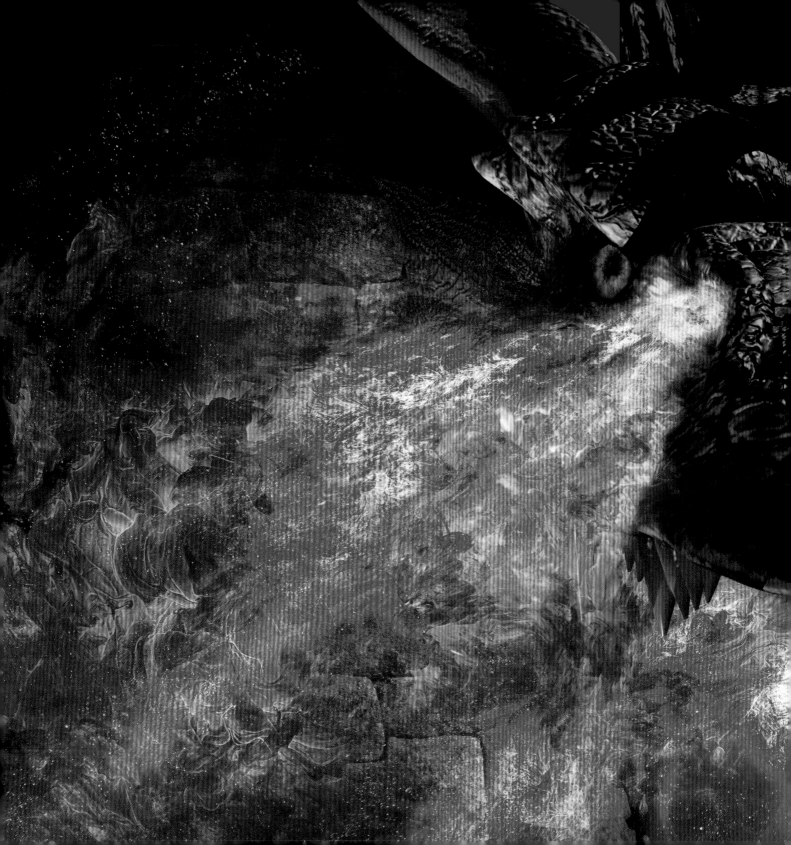

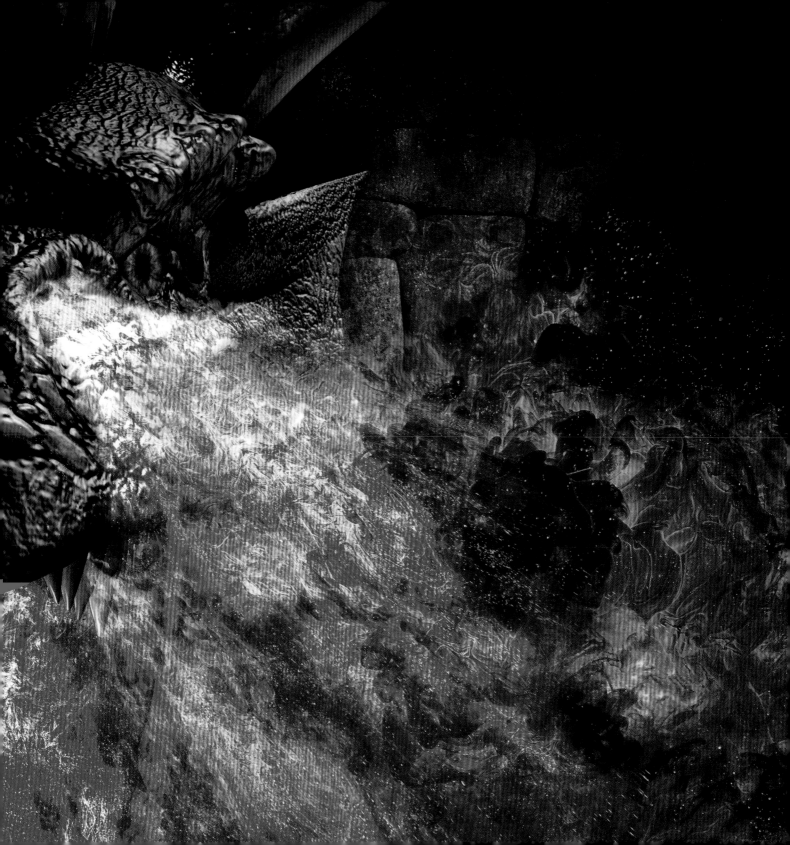

Acknowledgments

THIS IS A CARLTON BOOK

Text, design and illustrations
© Carlton Books Limited 2010, 2018

First published in 2010 under the title,
Dragonworld by Carlton Books Limited
An imprint of the Carlton Publishing Group,
20 Mortimer Street, London W1T 3JW
This edition published in 2018.

10 9 8 7 6 5 4 3 2 1

A catalogue record for this book is available from
the British Library.

ISBN: 978-1-78312-371-1
Printed in Heshan, China

PICTURE CREDITS:

The publishers would like to thank the following
sources for their kind permission to reproduce the
pictures in this book. Every effort has been made to
acknowledge correctly and contact the source and/or
copyright holder of each picture and Carlton Books
Limited apologises for any unintentional errors of
omissions, which will be corrected in future editions
of this book.

AKG-Images: /Erich Lessing: 66; Bone Clones, Inc.:
1TL, 1TC, 1TR, 1BR, 24-25, 33BR, 44-45, 67TR;
Getty Images: /Ira Block/National Geographic: 30-
31; /Don Mason/Corbis: 48; iStockphoto: 2-3, 68-69;
Lucyna Koch: 42-43; Natural History Museum: 28;
Photolibrary: /Mark MacEwan; Oxford Scientific:
37Russell Porter: 4-5, 15, 32, 33, 46-47, 64TL, 64BR

THE AUTHOR WOULD LIKE TO EXPRESS HER
SINCERE THANKS AND GRATITUDE TO THE
FOLLOWING ESTABLISHMENTS AND INDIVIDUALS,
WITHOUT WHOSE ASSISTANCE THIS BOOK COULD
NOT HAVE COME INTO BEING:

KEEPERS AND CURATORS of the Drachenfels teeth
collection, Bonn, Germany; The Wyrm Treasury, Krakow,
Poland; *Dr. Tiberius Pike*; Keepers of the Sumatran egg
collection, Padang, Sumatra; Members (living and deceased)
of the Drakon Expedition; *Stuart Martin* for his superb field
drawings, often made at considerable risk to his personal safety;
Jon Lucas and *Frank Denota* for their artistic vision;
Dud Moseley and *Carol Wright* for artistic support; *Jeff Shaw* for
dragon bone and teeth expertise; *Claire Hayward* for her print
expertise; and finally to my learned colleagues at the Ancient
Guild of Dragon Research, *Russell Porter* and *Barry Timms*, for
the benefit of their insight and considerable knowledge in this
most demanding of disciplines.